where do snowflakes go?

MW00966145

Story: Lyn Cook
Art: Rossitza Skortcheva

To Dashiell and Theo.

MOONSTONE PRESS

Design and imaging by Rossitza Skortcheva.
Typesetting and production by Tracey Rising.
Printed in Canada by Kromar Printing Ltd.

Moonstone Press books are published with financial assistance from
The Canada Council and the Ontario Arts Council.

Canadian Cataloguing in Publication Data

Cook, Lyn, 1918-
Where do snowflakes go?

Poem.
ISBN 0-920259-53-7

I. Skortcheva, Rossitza.   II. Title.

PS8505.065W4 1994   jC811'.54   C94-931427-7
PZ8.3.C66Wh 1994

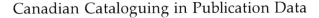

Moonstone Press
175 Brock Street
Goderich, Ontario
Canada N7A 1R4

for Rossi's family
for Matthew and Noah who began this story
for Kerry
from Rossi and Lyn
with love

The clock on the wall
Chimed half past eleven.
Time to tidy up and go!

"Don't forget your snowflakes,"
Miss Merry said.
They were big and beautiful,
All shapes, all colours.

It was Dad's turn to pick the boys up.
"Each snowflake is different,"
He told Matthew and Noah.
"Each one?" asked Matthew.
"Each one," Dad said. "Like yours and Noah's."
"Where do snowflakes go?" asked Matthew.
"They die," Noah said.
"They don't die," Matthew said. "They melt."

"They do die. They just die!"
"They don't. They melt!"
"Dad, where do snowflakes really go?"
"Everywhere," Dad said.
"They fall on the Arctic islands
Where the polar bears play,

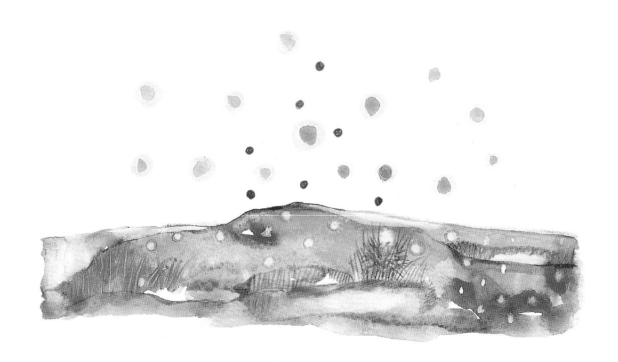

They fall on the mighty mountains
Where the eagles play,

They fall on the prairie lands
Where the gophers play,

They fall on the deep dark forests
Where the wild deer play,

They fall on the secret hidden places
Where the tiny creatures play,

They fall on the rivers
Rushing to the sea
Where the blue whales play.

And then, on a day when all the world is shining
The sun reaches down
And gathers them up to the sky again
To make a castle in the air.

And the castle grows and grows
Until the king of the castle cries,
'Enough! Let the snowflakes dance!'

And once again the snowflakes dance
And fall on the Arctic islands
Where the polar bears play,
On the mighty mountains
Where the eagles play,
On the prairie lands
Where the gophers play,

On the deep dark forests
Where the wild deer play,
On the secret hidden places
Where the tiny creatures play,
On the rivers rushing to the sea
Where the blue whales play."

"And on our own back yard
Where Matthew and Noah play!" said Matthew.
"Stay for lunch, Noah,
And we'll have fun in the snow."

"Because snowflakes don't die," Noah said.
"They have adventures everywhere,
And when they come home,
We make a snowman!"